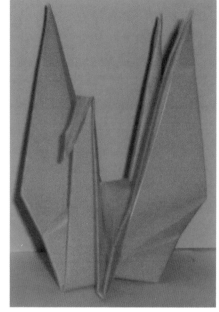

La Pajarita De Papel
The Little Spanish Folded Paper Bird

Collected Children's Stories

English Translations from Argentine Maria Luisa Leguizamón
by Edith Rusconi Kaltovich

ISBN 1-4196-0093-1

To order additional copies, please contact us.
BookSurge, LLC
www.booksurge.com
1-866-308-6235
orders@booksurge.com

The title "La Pajarita de Papel" is taken from a children's stories radio program in Córdoba, Argentina.

"Pajarita" or little Spanish bird, is the earliest recorded folded paper bird toy to emerge in Europe. The title of this collection of stories is a quotation from 1980 ORIGAMI PAPERFOLDING FOR FUN by Eric Kenneway.

Paperfolding "pajarita" by Masako Katsumata printed on the cover.

Reference: FALUCHO (called Antonio Ruiz): Pequeño Larousse Illustrated Dictionary Page 1288. Editorial Larousse Buenos Aires R13 Argentina

Illustrations by Gisela J. Bly.

Cover Design by ePrint Systems, LLC, Trenton, New Jersey.

A heartfelt thank you for Maria Luisa Leguizamón who contributed the Argentine Spanish Children's stories, and to all the participants who contributed and participated in the publication of this collection.

To our diverse and educated children of the 21st Century.

TABLE OF CONTENTS

Legend OF THE Dream

BY MARIA LUISA
TRANSLATIONS BY EDITH RUSCONI KALTOVICH

There is an island called Lemnos.

It is a very lonely island in the Egeo Sea in Greece. There lives a man called Sleep.

His house is a quiet cavern where everybody sleeps.

Everyone neither make noises nor speak aloud when they are

awakened. They are, of course, not accustomed to be awaked and they didn't know what else to do. This being the case, they did nothing but sleep.

That cavern was very dark because daylight couldn't reach there. It was impossible to guess whether it was day or night. The man named Sleep was not alone. He lived there with his children, big dreams, little dreams and his wife Night in his place. The big and little dreams were brothers and sisters.

The big dreams were tall and fat. They made strange noises when they were awaked. They disguised themselves as ghosts, wild animals and pirates.

The little dreams were small, short, and walked very fast. They were always joking and playing hide and seek. Sometimes, when they were bored, they took a walk around the island of Lemnos, where the garden of poppy flowers bloom in a variety of colors. Mother Night and father Sleep slept in the cavern. They wake up and go back to sleep. They go back to sleep and wake up again.

Days, months, and years go by this way.

Once one of the dreams, called Morpheus who was their god, ran away from the island. He was bored of sleeping all day, and traveled by train, motorcycle, airplane, and scooter.

He ate ice cream, lollipops, cookies, and mashed potatoes.

He heard the songs of the birds, the music of pianos, and even the noise of a child slurping his soup.

How happy he was when he returned to the island! He had so many things to tell … But he couldn't tell them because on the island, everything was quiet and sleeping, sleeping … ooh!… only sleep! Meanwhile, the poppies swayed back and forth pushed by the wind in the island's garden.

Morpheus felt the happiest of all the dreams on the island. He learnt the language of man and the thoughts of man's mind.

When Morpheus hears of someone who wants to sleep and cannot, who lives far, far away, he puts on his butterfly wings picks up the prettiest poppy flower from the garden and flies wherever he is called.

That is why, since Morpheus traveled around the Earth and he is being called by someone who wants to sleep and can't in spite of feeling very sleepy, he calls Morpheus.., Morpheus!.., until he closes their eyes. Then Morpheus' brothers and sisters, big dreams and little dreams come running to dance around the children to put them to sleep with the colorful poppies on the Greek island of Lemnos.

Mirandolina

by Edith Rusconi Kaltovich
and Maria Luisa

ILLUSTRATIONS BY Gisela J. Bly

My name is Mirandolina. I wear a dress of shiny, gray silver scales.

When I was very small, I played hide and seek with my brothers by swimming together in a school of fish and other water animals.

I swam very fast. I used to hide behind a coral-red reef or by the anchor hook near the square of my colony.

How blue everything was around me! It was a blue, pure and clear.

I grew up. One day, my mother told me that I was not a young silvery she-bass. That I could go swimming around the world because I could live in fresh or salt water.

"The world"! I exclaimed with wide eyes of pleasure and admiration.

I attempted to swim here and there, trying to get a view of my water-world. There were different water animals. Sometimes, they were smaller than me. Sometimes, they were bigger ones which seemed like giants to me. Some of them moved very fast, others moved very slowly.

I was curious. I was very curious. I discovered that some of my brothers whispered with their breathing gills and fins among themselves.

They told me stories with their mouths and nostrils about the times they went to see different worlds. The stories were not so much about the blue, pure and clear waters where we lived. If I asked them questions, they seemed cold-blooded and swam.

One of my cousins, who used to live in a colony of green algae, told me once that she ventured to go beyond the stream, far from her home. According to her, she'll never do it again because of the memory of such a shocking experience. She thought, she would never be able to return to her family and live in the floating green algae.

"What will there be beyond the blue, pure and clear waters that surrounded me? Who lives there? What color are the water animals there?", I asked myself.

One day, I separated myself from the group and drew apart from the main stream of the colony. Suddenly, I saw a graceful worm moving in front of me, very close to my nostrils.

If you only knew how much I like to eat little earth worms! I followed him without knowing that it was a fishing tackle! When I realized how far the little earth worm tackle had taken me. It was farther and higher than what I expected! It was moving to the rhythm and melody of our "arroz con leche" song. I was too far! I didn't want to lose him! I got closer and closer and he grasped my mouth! "How hard he is"! I thought to myself. "I've never eaten an earth worm like this one"! I tried to get loose, to run away but I couldn't. He seemed stronger than me! He dragged and pulled me! "Let him carry me"! I thought it would be safer for me. Suddenly, I felt a mouthful of cold strange air. I shivered!

"Could it be that strange air my friends inhaled and talked about"? I thought.

I remained hooked to the hard body of the tackle worm.

Suddenly, something grasped me firmly. It separated my mouth from the hook.

Enormous, round, hair eyes examined me. I did the same. How frightened I was! The owner of those eyes had no shiny, silvery scales, or fins, nor even a fish tail. Besides, nothing here was blue, pure and clear. Everything was green, brown or yellow.

I blew softly. My breathing became less frequent and more difficult from the exertion. Those very large hand fingers passed me to some else's fingers which manipulated me without pity. I was squeezed. They wrinkled the shiny, silvery scales of my dress.

"Was it the other world I wanted so anxiously to see"? Was it the world where everything was prettier and happier"? I asked myself.

In my confusion, I didn't know what to do. Suddenly, I felt the pressure of those fingers loosening themselves. I slipped through those fingers. I broke loose. I jumped. I got near the edge of the stream by the sand. I nearly fainted.

I jumped so high! I jumped again, again… and again until a jet of blue, pure and clear water went into my opened mouth! Finally, I gasped a deep sigh. I was able to breath again at ease!

I swam as fast as I could. I didn't stop until I arrived at the colony of green algae. Once there, I swam to my home.

"What a sense of relief! What a joy"! I was again in the blue, pure and clear water.

My mother looked at me. "What's the matter with you? Where did you come from"? She asked me.

I didn't want to tell her about my troubled adventure. I didn't want to worry her.

However, I want to tell you about my adventure, just in case you find me lost somewhere. Remember, I am Mirandolina, the gray bass fish with the shiny, silvery scale dress.

Please, put me back in my blue, pure and clear water.

PETER AND THE CAGED MOON

TRANSLATIONS BY EDITH RUSCONI KALTOVICH
ILLUSTRATIONS BY GISELA J. BLY

Once a child named Peter said that he wanted to hunt the moon and then put it in a cage.

Peter was 5-years-old with a tiny nose, a large swatch of hair that always covered one of his eyes, and dirty knees.

So, Peter went to hunt the moon.

"How proud this Peter is!" thought the butterflies, who heard about his wanting to hunt the moon.

"He wants nothing else but the moon" they said, "which is round like a ball…round, like a moon with a face covered with flour…white flour!"

The butterflies flew from flower to flower, from color to color, from flavor to flavor, without thinking to fly higher than the flowers in the garden.

Peter walked and thought about his vain idea. "Could he hunt the moon? Could he tie it up with a string, and put in a cage?"

There were rabbits in the back yard. They were eating carrots that were very tender. They passed hoppity, hop, by Peter's side. His knees were dirtier day after day; his nose smaller; and his swatch of hair did not cover one eye, but both!

The rabbits filled their mouths with carrots, looked at him and said: "How is he going to hunt the moon if he doesn't eat the raw carrots? He doesn't even have little round eyes!" Busily, they gnawed at the carrots.

Peter walked through the same paths over and over again. He played with a round ball, bouncing and bouncing. He whistled. He blew his swatch of hair covering his eye.

Once, Peter was told that ideas come like light blue clouds which float in the air, and when they knock at your head—"knock-knock"—they go into your mind until they are needed, and then, the idea, becomes true. That's why Peter walked through the same paths over and over again. He thought he might find the little, light blue cloud to solve his difficult problem. He expected that the little, light blue cloud could explain to a 5-year-old how to hunt the moon and lock it in a cage.

Around the corner, Peter met a salesman. A salesman of little, light blue clouds! Peter jumped with joy and happiness! He became so excited that he kissed everybody who passed by! He even wanted to eat raw carrots like the rabbits!

"Mr. Salesman!" he called. "Could you sell me a little, light blue cloud?"

The salesman looked at Peter and thought: "What a delightful child Peter is!" The salesman didn't even ask Peter if he had money to pay for the cloud.

"What type of little, light blue cloud do you need?" he asked.

He showed Peter what he had and said: "This one is for eating many sweets without upsetting your stomach. This one teaches how to solve arithmetic problems given by the teacher. This one, that is almost square, has a road inside which takes you to the circus. Which one do you want?"

Peter could have wanted the square cloud to laugh with the clowns, to admire the acrobats, to hear the roar of the tamed animals. No, he had made up his mind. He wanted the moon! He was not going to change his mind for a trip to the circus.

He approached the salesman of the little, light blue cloud and said: "I need a very special one, one which can help me to hunt the moon and to lock it in a cage, just like a bird."

The salesman looked through all the clouds. He looked, and he looked until he separated one of them very carefully. He folded it in four parts, wrapped it in tissue paper, and gave it to Peter.

Peter, who left his home without a penny and almost forgot to pay for the cloud, joyfully took off his pretty red tie and gave it to the salesman.

On his way back home, he ran without even watching the yellow, red, or green street lights at the corner, without seeing anybody, not even his friends, who looked at him with surprise and said: "Is Peter going mad?"

He was going mad with joy! He arrived home exhausted and speechless. He went into his room. He looked for his cage and sat down to wait in his small straw chair. He almost forgot the little package in his pocket. He took it out and untied it, smoothing the paper with his small hands. Peter kept it near him...he waited and waited once more.

The little, light blue cloud woke up and looked around. She saw Peter's swatch of hair, his tiny nose, and his dirty knees. She smiled at him and said: "Peter looks like an elf from the woods! He is so...,so pleasant!"

Peter took good care of her in his pocket, in a way that she didn't even get seasick.

The little, light blue cloud new that Peter's dream was almost impossible to be true. Nobody can hunt the moon because it is so very far away. It is very big. Suddenly, the cloud remembered that only once, a little, light blue cloud could please a child's dream. She wanted to please Peter, and so she did.

Peter, who was so tired, fell asleep.

When he woke up, the first thing that he did was to look at the cage. There was the moon! The moon was very quiet, white, and round, just as he used to see it from his window at night. What a joy for Peter! He smiled happily. How the children of the neighborhood, the butterflies, and the rabbits would envy him!

Peter smiled and smiled. He even imagined that the little white moon smiled at him, too!

There was only one thing that Peter never figured out. Because that night, although the moon was hunted and well kept in the cage, there was another proud and round moon coming out every night, rolling and smiling in the skies for him, he could even see her face when he looked out of the window of his room.

EL MONO MIRIKINA

BY
EDITH RUSCONI KALTOVICH
ILLUSTRATIONS BY GISELA J. BLY

Once upon a time, there was a grayish—or rather a mixture of very fine black and creamy white—hairy, long-tailed Mono, which in Spanish means "monkey."

He used to live in the forest of northern Argentina, in an area between Jujuy and Misiones. The small Mono Mirikina, as he is known, is a natural climber in his native country, where he likes to climb trees. One day, when Mirikina tried to leap into the branches of a tree, he wrapped his tail around his neck and almost strangled himself. He couldn't find a way to untangle his tail without hurting himself.

Many times his long tail got in his way when he walked. As he grew, his tail grew longer and skinnier, causing him more trouble.

Mirikina was upset because he couldn't control his movements as other monkeys did. The more he looked at his long tail, the more discouraged he became. The only solution was to hang his tail over a higher branch and sit on a lower one.

It was no easy life for Mono Mirikina. It wasn't dignified for a monkey; it just wasn't normal.

So, one day, he felt so badly dragging his long tail wherever he went, he considered having his tail cut off by the veterinarian at the zoo.

Mirikina went to the doctor's office, and with a smiling face complete with a set of large white teeth, he asked:

"Sir, could you please cut off this long, annoying tail?"

"Why?" asked the veterinarian. "I think you are a unique, attractive monkey with that unusual long tail."

"Oh, no!" cried Mirikina. "I want to get rid of this gross impediment. It makes me so unhappy."

"Very well," said the doctor.

He had never experienced this problem with monkeys in the zoo. He saw that Mirikina felt very badly, so he thought he'd better proceed to cut off his tail.

"Now, lie down on this table and we'll get ready to operate," said the veterinarian.

"Just a minute," said Mirikina. "Before you cut off my tail, I want to make a deal with you."

The doctor thought, what kind of deal could that be? After this operation I can keep this long tail as an exhibit and perhaps become a world-famous veterinarian. Then, when customers come to my office to have their pets' nails trimmed, the baby animals might not cry anymore because I would have an interesting exhibit to show them. So, he decided to listen to Mirikina's deal.

"In exchange for my tail," Mirikina said, "I would like to keep the sharp scissors you use to cut if off."

Mono Mirikina and the doctor agreed. He decided to give Mirikina the scissors in return for his tail.

The doctor turned towards his surgery tray. He put on his pair of rubber gloves, grabbed the pair of sharp scissors, the ones which he used to trim pet's nails. Mono Mirikina screeched. The doctor gave him some anesthesia to put him to sleep so it wouldn't hurt when he cut the tail. Mirikina didn't feel any pain when he woke up, he saw his tail sitting in a glass jar filled with alcohol. The veterinarian kept Mono's tail, and Mirikina kept the scissors.

Mirikina was so happy. He jumped off the table with the scissors in his hands, gratefully thanked the doctor, and left.

He walked for a long time because he felt so comfortable with a shorter tail. He didn't realize how far he walked that day.

For the first time, he felt really content without being hindered by his long tail. His first experiment was to see what happened when climbing trees, and how he could get down safely without hanging himself.

Mirikina was enjoying himself—no doubt about that. Then, suddenly, he saw two beautiful young girls cutting grass with their lovely hands.

"Hello, my name is Mirikina," said the monkey.

"Hello," answered the pretty young girls.

"You will ruin those hands if you keep cutting the grass that way," said Mirikina.

"What else can we do? There aren't any lawn mowers here," the girls answered.

"If you are willing to listen to me, I have a proposition for you," said Mirikina.

"What is it?" asked the young girls, excited to hear what this monkey had to say.

"I will give you my pair of sharp scissors, if you would give me a big plastic bag full of that nice green, tender grass," said Mirikina.

The young girls thought this was a good deal, giving away a big plastic bag of green, tender grass to Mirikina, if they could keep the sharp scissors. Imagine how quickly they could cut the grass now! So, Mirikina sat down under the shade of a tree to wait while the girls filled the bag with grass.

"Very well, Mirikina, you can keep this bag of grass, and we will use the scissors to cut the grass much faster."

Mirikina continued on his way happily, loaded down with the big bag of green, tender grass. This time he didn't walk too far. The bag was heavy and he got tired and hungry. He couldn't eat the grass. Monkeys only eat bananas.

Suddenly, Mirikina heard some crying. It was an old bread man, in his old-fashioned horse-drawn wagon, stopped along the side of the road.

"Why are you crying? Is there anything I can do for you?" asked Mirikina.

"I don't know," said the bread man. "My horse is so hungry! I can't sell enough bread to buy hay for him to eat."

"I don't have any hay," said Mirikina, "but I do have this bag of green tender grass that your horse can eat."

"Oh, thank you, thank you," said the old bread man, "but what can I do for you in return?"

"I could empty this bag of grass for you and fill it up with those wonderful, homemade hard rolls that you have in your basket. They look so good!"

"But, what will you do with so much bread?" said the bread man.

"Oh, I don't know. I'm very hungry, so I can eat some," said Mirikina.

They said good-bye to each other and Mono Mirikina kept walking along very happily, thinking of the good deed he had done by feeding that hungry horse. Mirikina thought of all the things that had happened to him since he had his long tail cut off: first the sharp scissors, second the bag of tender, green grass, third, this heavy bag of nice homemade rolls.

He sat at the edge of the road, eating a roll, just outside a nearby town. While he sat there, an elderly woman followed by many girls passed by. Because Mirikina didn't know how to count, he couldn't tell how many girls were in the group. But he remembered one, with a pretty chubby little face, sobbing very softly.

"Why is she crying?" Mono Mirikina asked the woman.

"There isn't enough to eat for all of us. I am a widow and I can't find work. We have very little to eat," she said.

"Don't cry any more, my dear," said Mirikina. "Here, here, have some delicious homemade rolls from my bag," and he handed the rolls to her.

"Thank you, thank you so much!" exclaimed the woman. "What can I do for you in return?"

"Well, let me think," said Mono Mirikina. "Since you are so poor, you could give me one of your daughters to keep me company."

"To lose one of my daughters! Oh, I couldn't do that!"

"But I will take very good care of her, and you will have one less child to feed," said Mono Mirikina.

The woman hesitated, giving this some thought. Finally, she agreed to give Mirikina one of the daughters. But she was careful to give him neither the oldest, nor the youngest, neither the prettiest nor the plainest, but one of the others—one with the pretty, chubby little face, who was still sobbing.

Mono Mirikina and his new found friend walked together hand in hand. As the first shadows of evening fell, Mirikina suggested that they should look for a house where they could spend the night.

By and by, they came to a small cottage sitting under the broad branches of a large oak tree.

The drab-looking door and windows were closed and dim. The house was built of dark-red bricks. The shingles, a dull color faded by the sun. The peak of the roof was outlined in white. The little front porch had three large windows, and a door opening onto it.

Mono Mirikina and the girl thought the house was abandoned and hesitated before knocking at the door. The flower beds were full of prickly stalks, and thistle-like plants blocked the entrance path. With a little of courage, Mirikina knocked at the door and someone answered in a very weak voice, "Come in, please." They stepped inside and found a very sick old man lying in his small bed. There were only a few things in the room: the old man's red tie, a little guitar hanging from a nail on one of the walls, and some dishes on the table.

They asked if they could help the old man, but he was so very sick that he could hardly answer. The girl went straight to work, cleaning the cottage, caring for the old man, and, when he smiled, Mono Mirikina realized how much the old man needed someone to help him.

Mirikina felt so happy since he had his tail cut off. He had done so many good deeds that he didn't even think of his long tail anymore. He turned to the gray-haired man and asked if he could play his guitar, and if he didn't mind, could he wear his red bow tie.

The old man smiled and nodded. Mirikina then smacked his lips and sang a song. He climbed to the top of the tree with such ease and confidence, as if he had been climbing that particular oak tree all his life and knew every branch and twig. His long hind legs never missed a sure resting place, and holding the guitar in his hands, he sang:

"Now, I sing under this oak tree
By-gee, all about my good deeds!
Hi-diddle dee, Hi-diddle,do
Now, I sing my own true tale:
I am here, I am Mono Mirikina
Who once had a long, long tail.
Hi-diddle dee, Hi-diddle do.
My tail made me so sad,
But now, I feel very glad!
Hi-diddle dee, Hi-diddle do.
I can sing under this oak tree
By gee, all about my good deeds!
Hi-diddle dee, Hi-diddle do . . . "

Gaillard the Pelican

by
Edith Rusconi Kaltovich
ILLUSTRATED BY GISELA J. BLY

My name is Gaillard. I took this name, Gaillard, after Wilson Gaillard, a dentist. He had the idea to make an island from a man-made dump in the middle of Mobile Bay in Alabama in 1982.

I, Gaillard, managed to make it off the extinction list.

I, Gaillard, made a frail come back from my ancestors because we were at risk on the list of extinction.

The main reason for my family's death was the pesticide DDT, a chemical preparation for destroying plants and animals pests. This pollutant poisoned my ancestors. It was poured into the air, beaches and rivers. It worked its way into their food system from their diet of dead fish.

My ancestors produced thin eggshells during their mating time.

My bird parents, with their web-feet, crushed and killed their offspring when they sat down to warm my sibling's eggs.

I was one of the blood-streaked eggs. I sat unattended for a whole month.

Like other birds, my parents didn't keep my egg warm enough for me to grow inside.

As I sat in the nest, I made light repeated jiggles to shake my egg. A minute later, I jiggled again. Then another jiggle until I cracked my eggshell. After many more cracks I split my shell until it was separated in two.

I was lying half inside my broken shell. Then—I hatched! I hatched!

My color was purple like a bruise, I shone like a wet eggplant. I was exhausted, ugly but cute. If you were to pick me up, you could cradle me in the palm of your hand.

I was only a minute-old pelican. My pop-eyed head appeared, creaking through my tiny bill—making sharp hissing sounds of happiness.

I struggle to cope with the awful stinking place where I was born during the early 1980's.

I call Gaillard Island my home, the birth place of my brand new life.

My home was a nest of broken reeds and dried crab grass in a messy place. Bird droppings and rotten fish covered the ground.

How it smells!

Here, the stink of sun-baked "guano," a name for bird mess, the stink of marsh muck, the stink of death, was too much for my beak and my stretchy pouch to bear.

There are dead fish all over, the food missed from mama's mouth to baby's mouth. Some greedy babies, are pushed out for all mama's attention and they starve to death. Dead pelican babies scatter around. Some fell out of their nests in the bushes and could not get back in. They died.

A lot of dead full-grown pelicans, wings outstretched, bodies disintegrating, littered my island.

Still a flightless baby in the scrub, I was hungry. I caught a large mullet, a kind of gray-reddish food fish, with two barbells on its chin. I had several inches of the mullet's tail sticking out of my mouth. I walked with it in my beak, but my beak is not made for carrying things. Well, I lifted my head, but the fish in my pouch would not slide down my throat into my stomach.

It was too big! I stuffed myself to the very brim. I was so hungry! I didn't want to throw back part of my catch. I got in my gulag pouch for a long time. The mullet's tail was hard and dry. Flies were buzzing around it. I dissolved the golden mullet's head. I digested it down my gullet leaving only the fish's tail still rotting in the open air.

By the time I was about three months old, I was ready to try flying. My first take off and landing were difficult. I awkwardly blundered up into the air and then belly flopped down into the water.

When I learned how to fly, I joined other pelicans in swooping and waving my 8-foot wingspan. I loved the diving and screaming with the flocks.

I was a very social bird with my slow, dignified flap, flap, flap and g-l-i-d-e.

Taking my cue from the one in front of me, I can move both my wings at the same time, passing the same flapping motion down the line in a continuous wave.

We travel one behind the other in a long trail, sometimes flying in a wide "V" formation.

Our noises make humans feel unwelcome.

I live surrounded with all kind of terns, a mixture of black-legged stilts, yellow crowned night herons, black egrets, laughing sea gulls, which flap, prowl and, yes, nest around me as well.

I have other friends like the nutria, a big rat like animal. It doesn't bother any of us birds, because it is a vegetarian rodent. Together with the nutria are raccoons, snakes, and possums who make the island a great place for us the pelicans and our babies to live.

My favorite place to sun is on top of a berm, a narrow shell patch along the top of a scarp, a side ditch next to the ring of rock rip-rap protecting Gaillard Island's shoreline.

Sometimes, I sit down in the scrubby bushes.

Sometimes, I sit on top of an old sign tossed ashore by hurricanes.

I, Gaillard, the pelican, am happy to live here. I don't complain about the blistering heat because I flutter the moist skin of my pouch moving the air around it. I use it as a way of keeping cool. My personal air conditioning.

I don't complain about the bad stink, the mosquitoes, the sand flies and other biting and stinging critters, not even that there's not a shade tree in sight on my island.

Perhaps the inhospitable nature of my place is responsible for the lack of tourist attraction, walkways, or organized tours for human visitors.

Today, I am a big, brown adult pelican. I've lost the ability to make noise, to muster the screechy hiss I made as a baby. I'm mute.

I soar with my powerful wings. I dive bomb into Mobile Bay. My great throat swells with water as I gobble up dinner for my babies.

BLACK BLUE FACHO

BY

EDITH RUSCONI KALTOVICH

Black Falucho was not my real name. It was just a nickname I gave myself later in life. My real name was Antonio Ruiz.

I lived in the outskirts of the Spanish-speaking community made up of the white upper class in Buenos Aires, Argentina.

I was called a "mestizo" because I was part white and part Indian blood. At the same time there were also the "mulattoes," who were part African and part Indian.

A large proportion of people of mixed blood became useful members of this community.

I was one of the very few mestizos or mulattoes who ever learned to read and write. People of mixed blood were legally excluded. Primary schools were few in number.

I found plenty to do growing up in Buenos Aires with a population of 70,000. It was a thriving town laid out on one uniform plan with streets running at right angles. In the center was the plaza, or open park about which were grouped the church, the "cabildo" or town hall, and the houses of the principal inhabitants. Less wealthy white families lived in the adjoining streets, and the "mestizos" and poor people generally, in the outskirts. In a town of this size, there were other churches in various wards, as well as a number of monasteries and convents.

As traveling became less difficult and costly, some of the wealthier "creoles" were able to go abroad. A few foreigners, including a small number of scientists and men of letters, came to Buenos Aires.

Unfortunately, I wasn't wealthy enough to go. However, the "creoles" who traveled abroad came into contact with the revolutionary ideas prevailing in the outside world, and some brought back books such as the works of Jean-Jeaques Rousseau, and newspapers disseminated his writings and prepared public opinion for outright independence. French encyclopedists circulated books secretly among their friends. Forbidden books like "The Rights of Man" stimulated not only other minds and my imagination all the more. If found in possession of them, people were severely punished.

I always said that I "owed everything" to my mother, black mulata, living in an adobe home. By her example, I had learned to be careful with money, when coins were introduced through the tobacco trade; to think of others before myself; and to love, love of country, of dear Buenos Aires, of family. Black mulata, my mother, had taught me well. She also fed me well too, with "mazamorra" or hominy, chocolate and "yerba mate" or Paraguay tea, which was consumed in great quantities in other River Plate provinces.

With my sense of love of personal freedom, I preferred to join, as many did, the first leader who promised a chance for excitement and plunder in a military campaign.

Once the British attempts were successfully repelled in the port city in 1807, the loosely-organized force already had its own elected officer corps, and I was receiving two hours of military training daily.

Even though I was freed from slavery by the Revolución de Mayo 25, 1810, referred to as the May Revolution, the governing Junta began to address the most important question posed in the viceroyalty.

I was so happy to see that the force had grown to a size of 8,000 men, roughly one-fifth of the total population of Buenos Aires. In the Defense, as the action subsequently became known, almost two-thirds of the militia were native born "criollos."

The colonial army posted at the city, depending on loyalty to the Spanish crown, were either dismissed or were reorganized into Buenos Aires' new military units, which were given such patriotic names as the "Dragoons of the Fatherland" or the "Artillery Men of the Fatherland". The Blandengues were renamed the "Mounted Volunteers of the Fatherland". Many Bladengues, however, resisted formal organization.

Most of Argentina outside the province of Buenos Aires, was by this time, controlled by the leaders of the "montoneras," undiscipline hords of "gaucho" cavalry, which began to appear on the pampas in the first years of independence. Freedom of trade had brought economic changes which made the gauchos' lot more difficult and which eventually compelled them to give up altogether their wild free life on the plains.

The presence of royalist forces elsewhere in the region, continued to threaten the new government's independence and prompted the creation of military units whose mission was to drive out the colonial army and its supporters.

I read about the territorial losses of Upper Perú and Paraguay, which prompted the fall of the junta and the appointment of the first Triumvirate on September 23, 1811. The Triumvirate instituted important changes through the creation of a Commission of Justice to deal with vagrants or "vagos" and delinquents and the establishment of a national library and schools.

I, Antonio Ruiz, who was a slave, fought against the British invasions with the popular militia, at an early age, and supported the cause of Independence during the May Revolution (May 25, 1810). In 1812-1813, I joined troops from Buenos Aires, led by General Manuel Belgrano, the creator of the Argentine light blue and white striped flag, who made a second effort to take Potosi and Upper Perú. I carried the Argentine flag during the early victories at Las Piedras, near Tucumán, and at Salta where General Belgrano gained another stunning victory over the royalists on February 20, 1813. He opened the way for an invasion of Upper Perú.

The militia and I often subsisted on meat "charque," "Tasajo" or beef jerky and "yerba mate" or Paraguay tea, an essential nutritional supplement to diets consisting solely of meats; and "mazamorra" or hominy, a kind of thick soup or boiled whole white corn.

By this time, I was growing up. I became a very tall young man. During the first period the Creole regime in Venezuela, New Granada (Colombia), Argentina and Chile, were simply struggling for existence, weakened by rivalries among leaders, and unable to win decisive victories over Royalists or Spaniards.

When I heard of volunteers joining the Argentine "Mounted Grenadier Regiment", I went to the headquarters to see General San Martín, who was organizing this army.

Early in 1813, Jose de San Martín distinguished himself by winning the battle of San Lorenzo, which drove the Royalists from the littoral provinces.

I insisted on seeing the General, who heard my voice outside his tent and asked me, "What can I do for you, young man? I'm the General."

"My name is Antonio Ruiz," I said. "I would like to join the Argentine Army."

"Very well," said the General. "You're enrolled and you can start your training now. I'll give you a uniform tomorrow."

The next day, when I saw the blue-and-white uniform, I tried it on. I felt so proud and elegant with such an unusual hat!

"Look at these two red feathered peaks on both sides of the hat!" I made the comment to other soldiers in the quarters.

"The hat is made of oilskin, a treated cloth that makes it waterproof and shiny," other soldiers explained.

"It is called a fa-lu-cho," said another soldier.

"What's a fa-lu-cho?" I asked.

"It's this special army hat that we wear with this elegant uniform," a soldier answered.

I tried the fa-lu-cho on. "How elegant I look!" I said to myself.

"I'm Black Fa-lu-cho from now on!" I said.

Since then, my real name of Antonio Ruiz was forgotten. Everyone called me "Black Falucho." So, I became one of the many dedicated soldiers of San Martín's troops.

I became so anxious to be ready for the regiment that I learned all the parts of the light blue-and-white Argentine flag. I repeated many times:

"the part of the flag attached to the staff is the hoist ... hoist."

The portion from the attached part to the free end is "the fly ... the fly."

I repeated: "Canton ... the canton ..." is the quarter part next to the staff and the top.

I also learned the rules and meaning of how and when to display the flag on different occasions during either peace or war.

I memorized about the flag being in front of the military right of the column, when placed with other flags in a parade, when on a wall with other flags, they have to be on its staff.

Meanwhile, I heard comments that the patriot movement was rising and falling in the north, a series of weak governments at Buenos Aires were endeavoring to liberate the rest of the territory of the former viceroy; with only partial success.

By then, the Argentine regime had somewhat more prestige and authority.

The war was renewed through the efforts of one determined leader: Jose de San Martín.

He obtained the governorship of Cuyo, today Mendoza, at the foot of the Andes.

I followed his plans for two years, in which I matured in the training of his troops.

Then it was when General San Martín put me in charge of the light blue-and-white Argentine flag. I was so proud that I even grew taller.

"You'll carry the flag through the passage of the Andes," he ordered.

The transportation of an army with its supplies and artillery over the passes, more than two miles above the sea level, was a notable feat.

"What a great deed!" I thought.

I, Black Falucho, followed the emblem through the roars of the battle of Chacabucho on February 12, 1817. I witnessed the battalions with swords and cannons. I descended the sides of the mountains in the western valleys. I defeated the Royalists. I forced them to evacuate Santiago, the capital of Chile. The Chileans received us with the enthusiasm of peace.

My emblem, through the smoke of the battle waved free, free, caressed by the Pacific Chilean Ocean breeze.

I let myself go and yelled: "VICTORY, VICTORY, holds you in my arms, now!"

But the battle was not over.

"I'll be with you, always with you, dear flag, I'll protect you from the enemy!"

The patriots' army was defeated by the royalists in the battle of Cancha Rayada in March, 1818. Three weeks later, on April 5, San Martín won the battle of Maipú. Since then the Spaniards didn't threaten central Chile again.

"Aren't you afraid to die?" some soldiers asked me.

"Am I afraid to die?" I answered with this question. I said: "I never feel death inside me. During the battles, I only know that I'm a Grenadier of San Martín's army!"

I marched proudly with the Argentine flag next to the white-and-red colors of the Chilean flag through the streets of Santiago. Two years later, preparations for the expedition northward were accomplished.

"How beautiful the crested waves of the Pacific Ocean greet us on our way!" I said. We landed in Pisco, south of Lima, Perú.

I, Black Falucho, was commanded to guard the Argentine and Peruvian flags. I was as dissatisfied as the Chilean troops, being under the orders of the Spanish enemy.

Callao, which was still held by the Royalists, later surrendered after a siege in which we, the defenders, endured ghastly sufferings.

I was guarding the Callao fort at the foot of the flagpole where the Argentine flag was, when a Spanish soldier forced me to surrender by changing the Peruvian flag for the red and yellow Spanish one. As I refused following his order, he said: "Look, soldier…your insane pride will cost you your life, you'll die!"

"Yes, I'll die as one of the heroes of this battle and as a Grenadier of San Martín!"

"Give up your pride and the Peruvian flag. You will die!" he repeated.

"My life is yours…I'm your prisoner. I lost my leader! Viva Buenos Aires!"

The Spanish enemy executed Black Falucho.

Since then, Black Falucho's name remained as an example of fidelity, not only to the Argentine, Chilean and Peruvian flags, but as one of the most heroic episodes in the Latin American struggle for independence from Spain.

EDITH R. KALTOVICH

Born in Córdoba, Argentina, Edith Rusconi Kaltovich received a M.A. from Mount Holyoke College. She uses her talents as a bilingual writer, poet and translator. After retiring from the Trenton Public School System, she became a Spanish professor adjunct at The College of New Jersey and Mercer County Community College in New Jersey.

She is the President of The New Jersey Poetry Society, Inc., active in PEN Women, World Poetry Society International, Mount Holyoke Princeton – Trenton Club, Delaware Valley Poets, Fernando Rielo Foundation, Spain – New York, The American Poetry Society, The Academy of American Poets, and Past President Arts Council Lawrenceville, New Jersey.

She had two books of poetry published, Brambled Thoughts While Trimming Mimosas and Other Poems and Harvest of Riches. Her published translated books include Romances to the Argentine Children; Collect Telegrams, Poems of Urgency; Message of Redemption; Mochito (Bilingual Children's Story); Selected Poems (Virgilio A. Olano B. – Colombia); and The Five Elements – An Epic (Krishna Srinivas – India) in Spanish.

Her name is listed in Who Is Who, in the International Poetry, Who Is Who in Public Affairs; Biographical Dictionary Universal International; Who Is Who in American Women, and Notable Americans of the Bicentennial Area (1976).

Member of the National Federation of States Poetry Society, Inc. The American Translators Association of New York, and The Association of Argentine Writers (SADE).

MARIA LUISA CRESTA de LEGUIZAMÓN

Maria Luisa Cresta de Leguizamón, Argentine, Professor at the National University of Córdoba, Argentina. A specialist in Hispanic American Literature, has published many essays on children's literature in her country and abroad. Author of many children's stories as well as her guidelines applied to children and adolescents.

MIRANDOLINA'S ADVENTURE and PETER AND THE CAGED MOON presented for the first time in a literary contest in the city of Azúl, Buenos Aires, Argentina received the Second and Fourth Place respectively in 1970.

EL MONO MIRIKINA received the 1st Place in the Children's Contest at the PEN WOMEN convention in Washington, DC in 2000.

BLACK FALUCHO was a finalist in the Council on Interracial Books for Children Inc., NY, NY in 1972.